Many thanks to the Rosenwach family
for providing blueprints of the water towers,
and for building them – R.C.

The Rooftop Rocket Party

For Finn and Jon

by Roland Chambers

Andersen Press
London

In the summer, Finn went to visit Doctor Gass in New York.

Doctor Gass was a famous Rocket Scientist.

But when Finn asked Doctor Gass where he *kept*
his rockets, the brilliant man just smiled and said:

"In a very secret and unusual place."

Rocket no. 34263

no.34264

Rocket no. 34265

Thrust   Direction

$E = MC^2$

Ink

There were no proper
rockets in Doctor Gass's
laboratory, which was green
and full of plans.

Or in his library,
which was red and
full of books.

FROM LAUNCH TO SPLASH DOWN

ROCKETS

ROCKET SCIENCE

ROCKET SALAD

COOKING IN DEEP SPACE

GETTING TO GRIPS WITH INFINITY

VA-VA-VOOM

APOLLO

ASPIRIN

ORBITS

ELLIPSES

COLLAPSES

THEORY

PLANETS

There were no rockets at all in Central Park, though Finn thought it would make a fantastic Launch Pad.

And although there were plenty in the Museum of Rocket Science, none of them belonged to Doctor Gass.

NASA

DO NOT TOUCH

Which was a pity.

That evening, over supper, Doctor Gass explained to Finn how the Moon moved around the Earth and was made of rocks.

"I always thought the Moon was made of cheese," said Finn.
"The Moon is a stone," said Doctor Gass.
"Then what does the Man in the Moon eat for his supper?"
wondered Finn.
"There is no supper on the Moon," said Doctor Gass,
"and what is more there is no Man in the Moon to eat it."
"Is that so?" said Finn.
"That," replied Doctor Gass, "is a mathematical certainty."

"Oh," said Finn . . .

. . . and went to bed.

But at twelve o'clock, when everybody was asleep,
a Night Thing came tapping at his window.
"Good evening," said the Night Thing. "My master is
the Man in the Moon and he has asked me to invite you
to his birthday party."

"But Doctor Gass says there is no Man in the Moon,"
said Finn.

"Is that so?" said the Night Thing.

"That," said Finn, "is a mathematical certainty."

The Night Thing just yawned and licked his chops.

"Twelve o'clock tomorrow night," he said, "don't be late."

The next morning Finn told Doctor Gass what he had seen.

"But that was just a dream!" said Doctor Gass.

And he explained how dreams worked.

And went on explaining until Finn begged him to stop.

That day they climbed the Empire State Building,
which was tall, but not *that* tall.

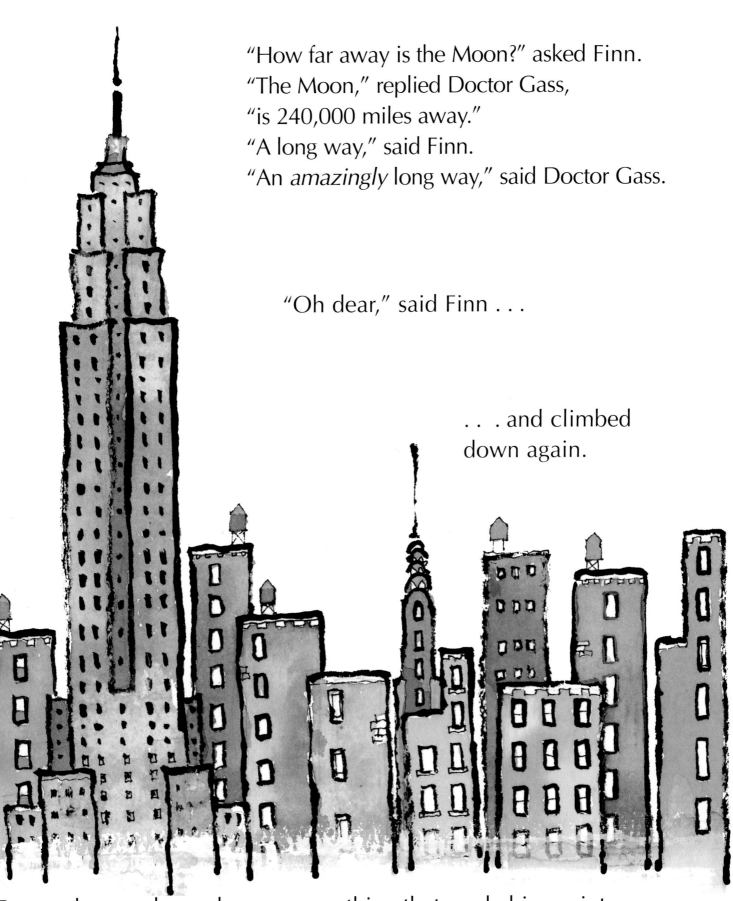

"How far away is the Moon?" asked Finn.
"The Moon," replied Doctor Gass,
"is 240,000 miles away."
"A long way," said Finn.
"An *amazingly* long way," said Doctor Gass.

"Oh dear," said Finn . . .

. . . and climbed
down again.

But on the way home he saw something that made him point
and shout, "Doctor Gass! I know where you hide your rockets!"

And there, on the rooftops, were big, red rockets, ready for lift-off!

"But those aren't rockets," laughed Doctor Gass,
"they're water towers!"

And he explained how water towers
held water to drink, and to shower
and to wash dishes now and then.

And he went ons explaining
until Finn begged him
to stop.

That evening, Finn asked Doctor Gass where he *did* keep his rockets.

"My rockets?" replied Doctor Gass, "Why, I keep them in the most secret and unusual place of all . . .

. . . my *head!!*"

Finn was so disappointed that he went to bed without touching his supper . . .

. . . which wasn't like Finn at all.

DO NOT DISTURB (EVER AGAIN)

But at five minutes to twelve the Night Thing
came tapping at his window.

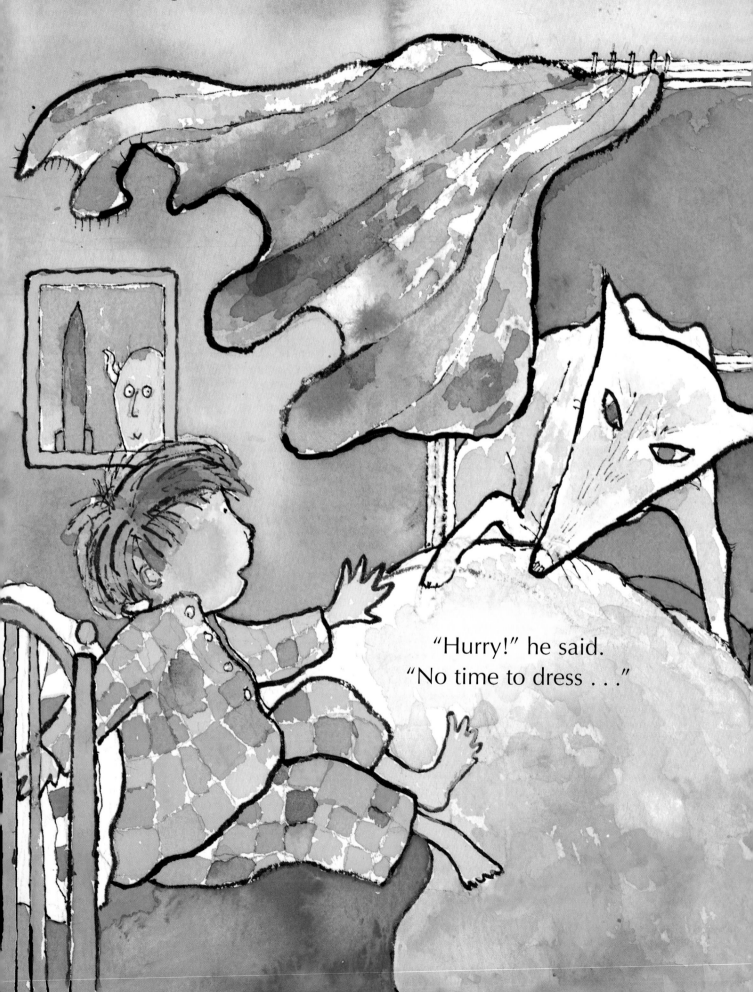

"Hurry!" he said.
"No time to dress . . ."

Up on the roof stood
the red tower.

"Just remember," said the Night
Thing, "every child in New York
has a rocket on his rooftop."

Lift-off!

Everybody was invited to the
Man in the Moon's birthday party.

When they landed,
the Man in the Moon met
them one by one.

"Good night!" he said,
"and welcome . . ."

"And now,
let the fun begin!"

First they played the bouncing game.

Finn bounced so high he thought he'd never come down again.

Next they hunted each other through the moon caves, which were all lit up with green.

When they were hungry they had a picnic. . .

. . . which tasted like nothing on Earth.

"But where is the cheese?" wondered Finn.

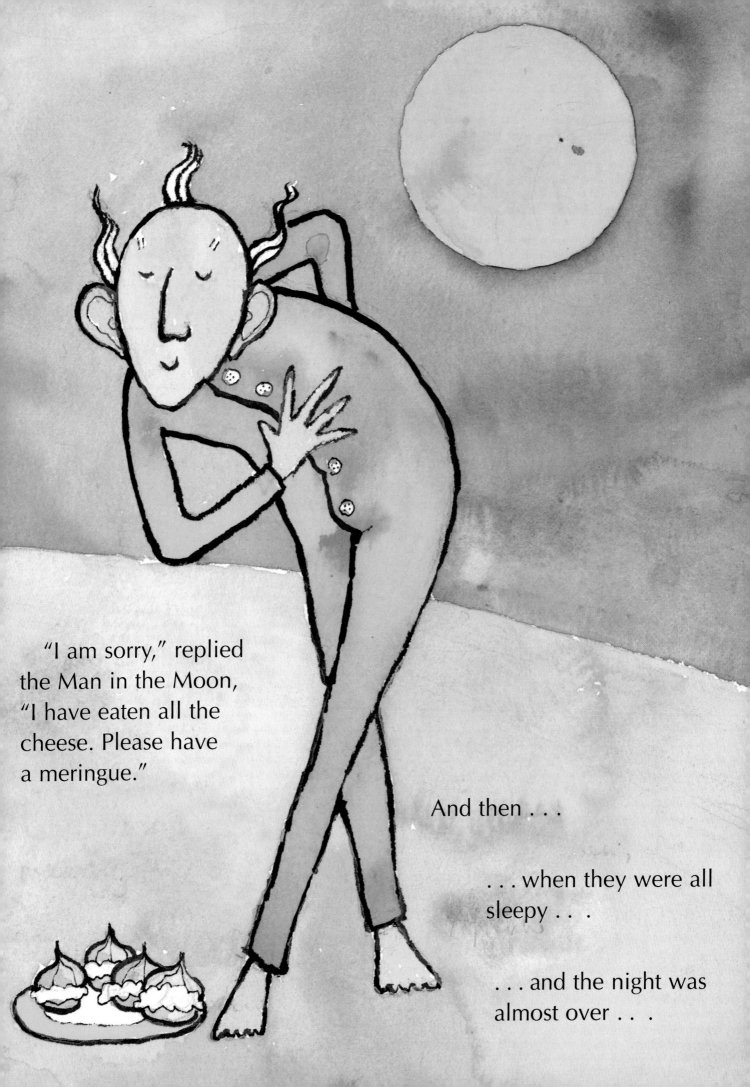

"I am sorry," replied the Man in the Moon, "I have eaten all the cheese. Please have a meringue."

And then . . .

. . . when they were all sleepy . . .

. . . and the night was almost over . . .

... the Man in the Moon played them a tune on his pale violin.

And then it was time
to go home.

The next morning Doctor Gass went
into his bathroom to brush his teeth.

But there was no water in the tap. Not a drop.

So he went outside in his
dressing gown to investigate.

And there he saw something so unmathematical . . .

. . . so *very* unscientific . . .

. . . that he closed his eyes and said, "RIDICULOUS!"

It was a great red rocket parked right in the middle of the street!

And close by, on the sidewalk,
was a half-eaten meringue . . .

. . . which belonged to a little boy
who was fast asleep upstairs . . .

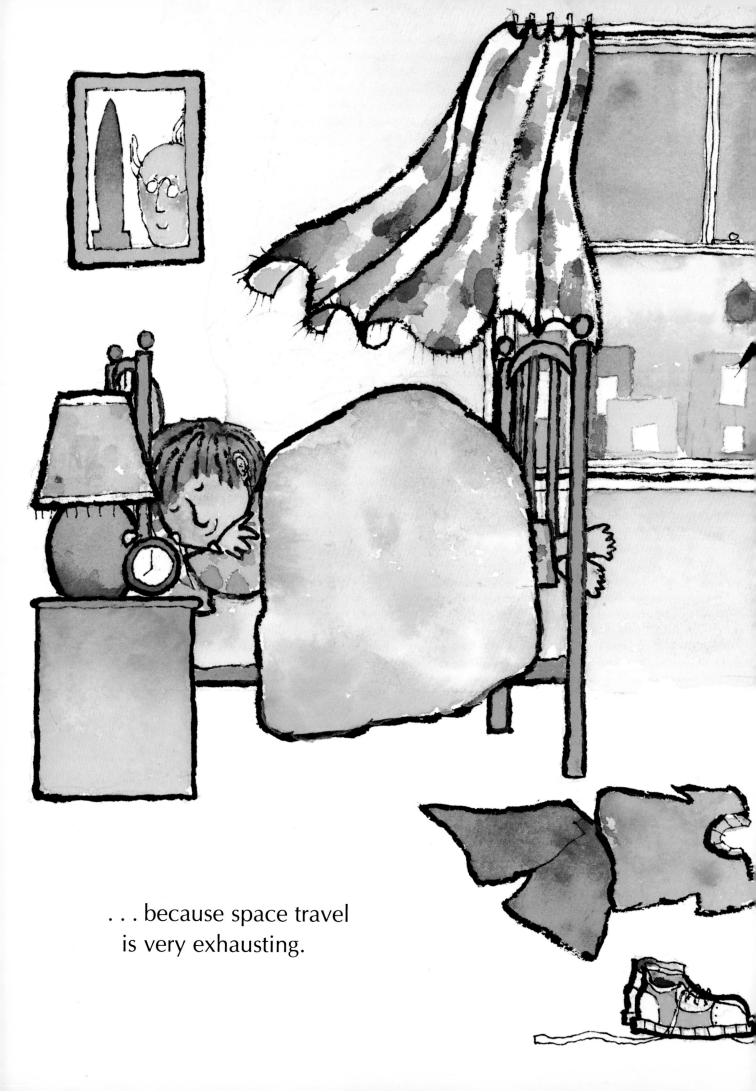

. . . because space travel
is very exhausting.